# BABY BABOON

Also by Mwenye Hadithi and Adrienne Kennaway

*Crafty Chameleon*
*Greedy Zebra*
*Hot Hippo*
*Lazy Lion*
*Tricky Tortoise*

First U.S. Edition

Published in Great Britain in 1993 by Hodder and Stoughton Children's Books

ISBN 0-316-33729-3

Library of Congress Catalog Card Number 92-56397

Library of Congress Cataloging-in-Publication information is available.

10 9 8 7 6 5 4 3 2 1

Printed in Belgium

# BABY BABOON

by **Mwenye Hadithi**

Illustrated by **Adrienne Kennaway**

Little, Brown and Company
Boston  Toronto  London

Baboon and Baby Baboon were playing
in a leafy tree outside Leopard's cave.

Leopard was hungry, but he was also lazy. So he lay silently in the tall, cool grass, with just the tip of his tail showing.

Soon Hare came hop-hopping along.
Leopard leaped up from the long grass
and chased Hare. He chased him and
chased him, backward and forward . . .

. . . until Hare ran down a hole in the riverbank.
   I've got you now, thought Leopard. And he hid
behind a big yellowbark tree, waiting for Hare
to come out again.
   He waited and waited.

Up in the tree, Baby Baboon laughed.
Leopard grew thirsty and tired of waiting.
He called to Baboon and Baby Baboon:
"I am going to the river for a drink. If you
will guard this hole for a moment and make
sure Hare does not come out, I will share
my dinner with you."

So Baboon came down and watched the hole. But while she watched, Hare ran to the end of the tunnel and dug his way out.

Leopard looked up just in time to see Hare
scampering away in the distance.
   And up in the tree, Baby Baboon laughed
and laughed.

Leopard was very angry.

"You let Hare get away," he roared. "I'll have to eat you instead."
So Baboon and Baby Baboon ran off, and Leopard chased them and chased them, round and round. Baboon ran to the top of a tall fever tree.

But Baby Baboon ran too slowly, and
Leopard caught him firmly by the tail.
And Baby Baboon didn't laugh. Not once.
"Help, help," he cried.

Now clever Vervet Monkey was also watching from the fever tree, and he called loudly to Leopard:

"Baboons are very tough to eat. But I can tell you how to make them as tender as the soft and delicious papaya fruit."

"How is that?" growled Leopard.

"You throw a baboon high-as-can-be in the air," suggested Vervet Monkey. "The more times the better. And soon the baboon will make a very tender, tasty snack."

"Well, they are extremely tough to chew," grunted Leopard. So he threw Baby Baboon high-as-can-be in the air and . . .

... just as he flew by, Baboon grabbed Baby Baboon and they went swinging away through the trees.

And Baby Baboon laughed and laughed.
And Leopard was angrier and hungrier than
ever. He ran after them and chased them, up
and down, but he couldn't catch them at all.

To this day, if you look carefully up in the tall trees, you may see Leopard lying in wait for Baboon.

And you just might hear Baby Baboon laughing and laughing.